TALES OF BUTTERCUP GROVE

Winter
Snow Fun

BY WENDY DUNHAM
ILLUSTRATED BY MICHAL SPARKS

HARVEST HOUSE PUBLISHERS
EUGENE, OREGON

The Scripture quotation on page 64 is taken from the *Holy Bible*, New Living Translation, copyright © 1996, 2004, 2007, 2013 by Tyndale House Foundation. Used by permission of Tyndale House Publishers, Inc., Carol Stream, Illinois 60188. All rights reserved.

Cover design by Mary Eakin

Interior design by Janelle Coury

Published in association with the William K. Jensen Literary Agency, 119 Bampton Court, Eugene, Oregon 97404.

HARVEST KIDS is a registered trademark of The Hawkins Children's LLC. Harvest House Publishers, Inc., is the exclusive licensee of the federally registered trademark HARVEST KIDS.

WINTER SNOW FUN

Copyright © 2018 by Wendy Dunham
Artwork © 2018 by Michal Sparks
Published by Harvest House Publishers
Eugene, Oregon 97408
www.harvesthousepublishers.com

ISBN 978-0-7369-7207-9 (hardcover)
ISBN 978-0-7369-7208-6 (eBook)

Library of Congress Cataloging-in-Publication Data
Names: Dunham, Wendy, author. | Sparks, Michal, illustrator.
Title: Winter snow fun / Wendy Dunham ; illustrations by Michal Sparks.
Description: Eugene, Oregon : Harvest House Publishers, [2018] | Summary: Skunk and Raccoon patiently wait for winter's first snowfall, then invite their friends over for a day of fun.
Identifiers: LCCN 2017038284 (print) | LCCN 2017048234 (ebook) | ISBN 9780736972086 (ebook) | ISBN 9780736972079 (hardcover)
Subjects: | CYAC: Snow—Fiction. | Friendship—Fiction. | Animals—Fiction. | Winter—Fiction.
Classification: LCC PZ7.1.D86 (ebook) | LCC PZ7.1.D86 Wit 2018 (print) | DDC [E]—dc23
LC record available at https://lccn.loc.gov/2017038284

Printed in China

18 19 20 21 22 23 24 25 26 / RDS-JC / 10 9 8 7 6 5 4 3 2

1

Waiting for Snow

Skunk and Raccoon sat on a rock.
It was very cold.

They had on their mittens.
They had on their hats.
They had on their scarves.

They sat and waited.
And waited. And waited.

"It will never happen," said Skunk.
"It will never snow."

"Do not worry," said Raccoon.
"It will snow."

"Okay," said Skunk. "I will keep waiting."

Skunk and Raccoon waited all day.
The sun went down, and it grew dark.
But there was no snow.

"Now it is time for bed," said Skunk.
"I told you it would not snow.
It will never snow."

Raccoon patted his friend on the shoulder.

"Do not give up," said Raccoon.
"Tomorrow we will wait again.
It will snow soon."

Skunk and Raccoon walked to their
homes. They both put on their pajamas.
They both climbed into their warm beds.

And they both had dreams about snow.

2

Snowy Surprise

Skunk was first to wake in the morning. He looked out his window. He could not believe his eyes.

There was snow. All the grass was white.

Skunk hurried to his phone. He called
Raccoon. "Good morning, Raccoon," he
said. "You were right. It did snow!"

Raccoon looked out his window and smiled. "Let's call our friends," he said. "We will have a fun day in the snow. We can meet at my house."

Skunk called Mouse, Mole, and Beaver.
Raccoon called Fox and Rabbit.

Soon everyone was at Raccoon's house.

"What should we do to have fun?" asked Skunk.

"We could go sledding," said Mouse.

Skunk shook his head.

"We cannot go sledding.
We do not have a big hill to slide down."

"But we can make one," said Raccoon.
"If we work together, we can make a very
big hill."

Skunk, Raccoon, Mouse, Mole, Beaver,
Fox, and Rabbit all worked together.
They carried buckets of snow from
all over Raccoon's yard.

They dumped it in one big pile.

They worked for a very long time.

After they had enough snow, they shaped it into a big hill.

Everyone climbed to the top. They slid down one at a time. They slid down in pairs. They hooked their legs together to make a train.

They were having a fun day in the snow.

3

Hello, Sun

Soon the snow clouds blew away and the
sun came out. The sun made the snow soft
and wet.

"Oh dear," said Skunk. "Now it is warm, and the snow is melting. Sledding is over. Now our snow fun is done."

"Our snow fun is not done," said Raccoon. "Now the snow is perfect to make a snowman."

Skunk and Raccoon worked together.
They rolled a big ball of snow for the
bottom.

Fox and Rabbit worked together.
They rolled a medium-size ball of snow for
the middle.

Beaver rolled a smaller ball for the head.
He set it on top.

Mole found two sticks for the arms.
Raccoon helped poke them where they
belonged.

Mouse found two small rocks for the snowman's eyes. He found more rocks for the nose and mouth.

Skunk lifted Mouse so he could reach the top. Mouse made the snowman a happy face.

Everyone stood back and looked at the
snowman.

"He is a nice snowman," said Skunk.
"But he is missing something."

"He needs a hat," said Mole.

"And he needs a scarf," said Beaver.

"He needs mittens too," said Mouse.

"It is warm out now," said Raccoon.
"I do not need my hat."

Raccoon put his hat on the snowman.

"And I do not need my mittens," said Fox.
So Fox put his mittens on the snowman.

"I do not need my scarf," said Mouse.
"But my scarf will be too small for the
snowman."

"You are right," said Raccoon. "Your scarf is too small."

Rabbit took her scarf off. "We can use mine," she said. Then she wrapped her scarf around the snowman.

"We finished the snowman just in time,"
said Skunk. "The snow is melting fast.
The grass is showing. Now our snow fun is
really done."

"It is not done," said Raccoon. "We can
go in my house and have more fun. I will
make hot chocolate with marshmallows."

Everyone went inside Raccoon's house.
They sat around the fireplace and drank
hot chocolate.

4

Snowball Fight

"That was a fun day in the snow," said
Raccoon. "We made a big hill. We went
sledding. And we built a snowman."

"I wish the snow didn't melt," said Skunk.
"We could have had a snowball fight too."

Raccoon had an idea. "We still can," he said. Raccoon reached into the bag of marshmallows.

He threw a marshmallow at Skunk.

He threw a marshmallow at Fox.

He threw a marshmallow at Rabbit.
He threw a marshmallow at Beaver.

Each of them threw the marshmallows
back at Raccoon.

Marshmallows flew everywhere. They
laughed and laughed until their bellies
hurt.

The marshmallows were too big for Mouse and Mole. They stayed under the table, where they were safe.

Raccoon gave them marshmallows to
jump on.

Mouse and Mole jumped up and down on their marshmallows. They were laughing too.

"This is fun!" shouted Skunk. "It feels good to laugh!"

"You are right," said Raccoon. "It is great
fun to laugh!"

"A cheerful heart is good medicine."

Proverbs 17:22